The King's Warrior

A Story of Ancient India

by Jessica Gunderson

illustrated by Caroline Hu

PICTURE WINDOW BOOKS
Minneapolis, Minnesota

Editor: Julie Gassman
Designer: Hilary Wacholz
Art Director: Heather Kindseth
Managing Editor: Christianne Jones
The illustrations in this book were created with
brushed pen and ink.

Picture Window Books
151 Good Counsel Drive
P.O. Box 669
Mankato, MN 56002-0669
877-845-8392
www.picturewindowbooks.com

Printed in the United States of America.

Library of Congress Cataloging-in-Publication Data
Gunderson, Jessica.
The king's warrior/ by Jessica Gunderson; illustrated by
Caroline Hu.
p. cm. — (Read-it! chapter books. Historical tales)
Includes bibliographical references.
ISBN 978-1-4048-5228-0
1. India—History—To 324 B.C.—Juvenile fiction.
2. Asoka, King of Magadha, fl. 259 B.C.—Juvenile
fiction. [1. India—History—To 324 B.C.—Fiction.
2. Asoka, King of Magadha, fl. 259 B.C.—Fiction.]
I. Hu, Caroline, ill. II. Title.
  PZ7.G963Ki 2009
  [Fic]—dc22
                                    2008032421

Table of Contents

Words to Know

admiration: a feeling of great respect or approval

admired: liked and respected

conquer: to beat and take control of an enemy

defeating: beating someone in a war or contest

emperor: the ruler of a group of lands

empire: a group of lands with the same ruler

outcaste: one who has no caste, or class

previous: happened before

reluctantly: unwillingly

surrendered: gave up or admitted that one has been beaten in a fight

Pronunciations

Asoka: ah-SHOH-kah

Buddhist: BOO-dist

Chandragupta: shahn-druh-GOOP-tah

Hindu: HIN-doo

Hinduism: HIN-doo-izm

Kalinga: kah-LIN-guh

Magadha: MUH-guh-duh

Nandi: NAHN-dee

Talik: tah-LEEK

Tungar: TOON-gar

Ved: VED

India, 262 B.C.

I was a warrior for the great king Asoka, but not just any warrior. I was on my way to becoming the world's greatest!

I was just a boy. But Asoka noticed me among the many other warriors in his army.

Asoka walked through our ranks every day, inspecting us. He often spoke to me, and today was no different.

"Tungar," Asoka said, looking me up and down. "You are fearless and heartless. Qualities of a great warrior."

The other boy warriors looked at me with envy. What could I say? I was the best warrior in the empire. They could never even come close to my greatness.

"I will fight for you, my king," I told Asoka.

But I knew it was not true. I would not go into battle for Asoka. I would go for myself, for the glory. My greatest dream was to become the youngest general in Magadha, the heart of the empire.

After Asoka had passed by, Nandi, one of the other boy warriors, came up to me. "What did you do to get Asoka's attention?" he asked. Nandi admired me and often followed at my heels like a dog. He wanted to be just like me, but he never would be.

I would tell him my story. But first, I straightened my sword and tightened my gold belt. I raised my shield and looked into it. I could see myself, a handsome, fierce boy. Several other boys gathered near, wondering what I was doing.

"Well?" Nandi persisted. "Tell us why Asoka chose you to ride next to him in battle. Tell us the story!"

I could never pass up a chance to tell the tale. After all, it was a wonderful story, even if parts were lies.

"I have saved Asoka from death many times," I began. "Once, he was walking through the trees alone. He was deep in thought. He didn't notice the tiger crouched, and ready to pounce. But I saw the beast. I raised my spear . . ."

I paused. Or was it an arrow? I had told the story many times, but I couldn't remember.

The boys were waiting for me to finish. One boy, Ved, tapped his foot impatiently.

"Tungar!" King Asoka interrupted, walking toward us. "I am meeting with the generals, and I want you there. You are a smart boy. You can give me your youthful wisdom."

"I am not a boy. I am a warrior!" I lifted my chin proudly. The other boys were shocked. None of them would dare to speak to the great Asoka that way.

Asoka frowned. "Very well then, warrior." He sounded displeased, but I was not worried. I followed him to his tent.

"I am going to begin another conquest," Asoka said when the generals had gathered. "We will conquer Kalinga."

The generals muttered in surprise. "But Kalinga is a strong kingdom! If we try to conquer it, many people will die," General Talik warned.

Asoka frowned. "Anyone who does not follow me will be fed to the elephants!"

"But Asoka, elephants don't eat meat!" Talik replied.

I put my hand on my sword, glaring at Talik. "Shall I kill him and take him to the elephants, my king?" I asked.

General Talik laughed.

"Quiet!" shouted Asoka. "Tomorrow we will go to Kalinga."

"I will join you, my king," I said. "I am fearless and brave!"

I tried to ignore the chuckles of the generals. They thought I was just a boy, but they were wrong. They would see. Soon I'd be a greater general than any of them.

CHAPTER TWO
The Untouchables

Our army headed south toward Kalinga. The ground rumbled under the hooves of our army horses.

Asoka rode on an elephant near the front of the army. The other boy warriors were in the rear, but I rode up front near Asoka. Ved's jealous eyes and Nandi's admiring eyes were at my back.

"Why must we keep fighting other kingdoms?" asked General Talik.

"My grandfather, Chandragupta, conquered many kingdoms. And I will do the same!" answered Asoka.

"Chandragupta was the greatest emperor of Magadha," I said.

"I know that!" General Talik
exclaimed. "I don't need a boy to tell me."

But I had a feeling he was lying. Even
though I was a boy, I knew much more
than Talik. And I would become a much
better general than he ever was.

"The boy knows much," General
Talik laughed. "Where did you find him,
Asoka?"

"A child's wisdom is good to take to
battle," Asoka said. "My grandfather
once said that his boy soldiers helped
him conquer many lands."

"You shouldn't compare yourself to Chandragupta," I told Asoka. "You are a much better king than he was!"

I had meant my words to be praise. But Asoka did not look pleased. "Tungar, remember that you are speaking about my grandfather."

"Sorry, Asoka."

He glanced behind him. "Where are your friends, Ved and Nandi? Bring them to me."

"They are not my friends. And they are not worthy of you."

"Do as I tell you!" cried Asoka.

I had no choice. If I wanted to become a general, I must first learn to obey.

Along the way, villagers had gathered to watch us go by. I waved to them.

A small boy and his father stood apart from the other villagers.

I looked away quickly. The boy and his father were Untouchables, or Outcastes.

I followed the Hindu religion. Hindu followers believe that people are born into castes, or classes.

Untouchables were so low that they did not even have a caste. Touching them or even looking at them could make you unclean.

I shivered, wishing I hadn't seen them. They might bring me bad luck.

I reached Ved and Nandi. "Asoka wants you to join him," I said reluctantly.

Ved looked like he had been expecting Asoka to call for him. But Nandi was so surprised he almost fell over.

Asoka turned to us as we approached. "Ved, are you afraid of battle?"

Ved puffed up his chest. "No," he answered.

"Tungar, are you afraid of battle?"

I puffed up my chest and stood taller than Ved. "No."

"Nandi, are you afraid of battle?"

Nandi looked from us to Asoka. Then he lowered his eyes. "Yes," he admitted.

Asoka grinned and patted Nandi on the back. "Good! Fear is the sign of a true warrior. Nandi will ride with me into battle."

"But you said a warrior should be fearless!" I cried.

"I have changed my mind. Now, Tungar and Ved, go back to the other boys."

When we returned, the other boy soldiers made fun of me. "Poor Tungar. No longer Asoka's little general!"

I ignored them. They were just jealous, as usual. One day I would be a general. Then they would have to obey me.

But now I was angry and confused. Why had Asoka changed his mind?

The Untouchables! It was true. They really had brought bad luck.

After many days, we reached Kalinga.
Their soldiers were ready for us. They
fought hard, and the war lasted many
weeks. I hadn't seen Asoka or Nandi
since we arrived in Kalinga. Asoka could
not see my brave fighting.

"What brave things have you done?"
Ved asked one night. The battle had
slowed, and we were resting in our camp.

What had I done? I thought fast. "I
got two Kalinga soldiers to fight each
other," I said. "They both rushed at me.
But I ducked, and their swords hit each
other."

"Then what happened?" asked one of
the boys.

I was usually good at inventing
stories. But now nothing came to mind.

"I don't know. I ran away," I said.

"You ran away?" asked Ved. "A general never runs away."

The next day, rain fell thick and fast. The fighting was slow.

Feeling tired, I found a quiet shrub away from the battlefield. I pulled my shield over my head and fell fast asleep. But soon I was awakened by shouts. "Help!"

The voice was familiar. "Nandi!" I cried, leaping up.

I saw him lying face-down on a hill nearby. The slippery mud was pulling him toward the edge of the cliff.

"Nandi! Get up!" I ordered.

"I can't," he said.

Running toward him, I saw why he couldn't move. He was holding onto the hand of a little boy. The child was dangling over the edge of the cliff.

The boy flapped his legs. He looked up at us, frightened.

His face looked familiar. Where had I seen him before?

"Help us, Tungar!" Nandi pleaded. "You are brave and strong."

I rushed to Nandi's side. While Nandi gripped one of the boy's hands, I grabbed the other. Together, Nandi and I pulled and pulled.

My hands were slick with mud and rain. I felt the little boy sliding away. But I tugged with all my might. The mud slurped as I pulled the boy onto the hill.

He stood up and wiped his muddy face. "Thank you," he said, turning to run away.

"Wait!" I said.

Nandi tugged my arm. "Did you hear that?" he whispered, glancing behind him.

A rustling sound was coming from the bushes behind us. I turned and looked, but no one was there.

"It's just the rain," I said. I turned back to the boy.

Nandi tugged my arm again. "Let's go." He looked like he didn't want to be near the boy.

Suddenly I remembered where I had seen the child. He was near the road as the army passed. He must have decided to follow us.

He was the Untouchable. An Outcaste. Because I touched him, I would be unclean forever.

"You knew!" I accused Nandi as we walked back toward camp.

Nandi shrugged. "I couldn't let him fall. He's just a little boy."

"He's an Untouchable!"

"It's not his fault that he was born an Untouchable," Nandi argued.

"Untouchables are outcasts because they did something bad in their previous life. They are dirty. And now we are, too!"

We made our way toward the camp. We could see the Kalinga city was burning. Smoke rose. Shouts filled the air.

Kalinga had surrendered.

Ved was grinning when we reached the camp. But it wasn't because we had conquered Kalinga. He had a look in his eyes like he knew something. The sound in the bushes! Had Ved seen us with the Untouchable?

When we walked past him, he jumped backward as though he didn't want us to touch him.

"Tungar," Ved sang. "You used to be so brave and so handsome. You were going to be Asoka's great general. But now you are unclean."

I glared at him. "I don't know what you are talking about," I lied. "And you will never become a general. You have done nothing worthy enough."

"At least I haven't done anything unworthy," Ved said.

I shot a look at Nandi, who didn't seem concerned. But he wasn't the one who hoped to be Magadha's youngest general.

I walked to the edge of the hill to look at the city burning below. Thousands of enemy soldiers lay dead. Thousands of others were being led away as prisoners.

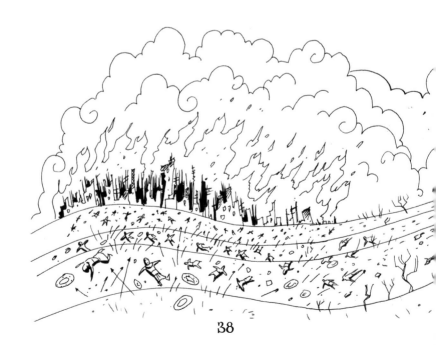

Pride swelled in me. Because of
Asoka and our army, Kalinga had been
conquered.

I heard a sniffle behind me. Nandi
had followed me again. A tear rolled
down his cheek as he stared at the
burning city.

"Silly Nandi!" I scolded. "We have
done our mission. We've conquered
Kalinga. Why are you crying?"

"It's just smoke in my eyes," he said, turning his face away.

If only Asoka could see him now! Then he'd know who deserved to ride next to him. He'd know who deserved to become a general. Not poor, sobbing Nandi.

Below, Asoka was riding through the destroyed city. He looked around him at the burning buildings.

I scrambled down the hill toward Asoka. Nandi was behind me, of course. My faithful little puppy dog! "Shoo!" I said, but he kept tagging along behind me down the hill.

I marched toward Asoka. "Do you see, Asoka? We've conquered Kalinga!"

Asoka was silent. He gazed at the smoking buildings and the women crying over their husbands and sons.

He looked around the city. The smoke
and destruction were reflected in his eyes.

"What have I done?" Asoka whispered.

"You have become an even greater
king!" I exclaimed.

Asoka shook his head. His eyes
drooped with sadness. Then he threw up
his hands and raised his head.

"What have I done?" he roared.

His voice echoed through the
destroyed city.

For once I had nothing to say.

CHAPTER Five
Truth and Lies

"We should no longer talk to Asoka," Nandi whispered. "We are unclean."

"Even an Untouchable won't make me unworthy of Asoka." I said.

But I wasn't as sure as I sounded. As we climbed back up the hill, I felt Ved staring at us.

"Tell us your battle stories, Tungar," Ved called. His eyes glittered. "Any feats of bravery?"

All I could think about is how I saved Nandi and the little boy. I had been brave, hadn't I? Even though the Untouchable didn't deserve my help, he was alive because of me.

"I saved ... Asoka!" I boasted. The words flew out of my mouth before I could stop them. "He was stuck in the mud, sliding toward the edge of a cliff."

"And then I rushed to help him!" Nandi interrupted. "But I slipped in the mud, too. Tungar appeared just in time." Nandi looked at me. He was hoping to win my admiration.

I couldn't believe it. Honest Nandi. Now he was lying, just like me.

What have I done? Asoka's words echoed in my brain.

"I pulled them both out of the mud. End of story," I said.

"Are you sure it was Asoka you saved?" Ved asked.

"How could I mistake our king? He is what I live for."

Ved shook his head. "You have lived your whole life for Asoka. You treat your friends badly," Ved gestured toward Nandi.

"I have no friends!" I said. "I have only a little puppy dog who follows me around." I tried to ignore the hurt look in Nandi's eyes.

Asoka was not himself after defeating Kalinga. We returned to the palace in Magadha, but Asoka did not throw any feasts.

Instead, he gathered Buddhist priests to him. The priests were known for teaching about peace. They spent many days alone with Asoka.

Then one day Asoka called a meeting of his soldiers. Because there were so many of us, we met on a small hill outside the palace. My heart raced.

Maybe today Asoka would make me the youngest general in Magadha!

"Soldiers, you have been faithful and courageous," Asoka began. "But I no longer need an army."

The soldiers muttered among themselves. General Talik stared at Asoka.

"You will conquer no more kingdoms," said King Asoka. "Instead, you will be put to work planting trees and fruit orchards. You will build wells and roads."

What glory was there in building a well or planting a tree?

"From now on, I will be devoted to making life much better for my people. All my people, even those in the lower castes," said Asoka.

The army grumbled even louder.

Asoka raised his hands to silence
them. "I deeply regret the lives lost in
Kalinga. Because of me, many people
are dead."

I stepped up to him. "There is a story in our great poem," I said.

Asoka frowned, but I kept going. "In the poem, a warrior feels bad for taking human life in battle. Then a god comes to him. The god tells the fighter that he was born to be a warrior."

"He must live a warrior's life with no regrets. The lesson is that we should accept the lives we are born into."

Asoka said nothing.

"You see. You are like the warrior! You must accept that," I said.

Asoka shook his head. "This poem has many great lessons. But I have learned my own lesson. People should not die because of me."

What was Asoka thinking? If he did not continue to conquer other kingdoms, he would never be remembered as a great king.

And I would never become a great general.

CHAPTER Six
Nandi's Reward

I heard a noise in the bushes beside me. A face was peering at me through the leaves. The Untouchable! I turned away with disgust.

And then I was staring into Ved's smirking face.

"Did you find your friend?" he said, pointing at the little Untouchable boy.

I did what I always do in times of
trouble. I raised my shield and looked
at my reflection. But I no longer saw a
handsome, brave boy. I saw only a lying,
selfish boy.

"King Asoka!" Ved called. "I think
Tungar has something to confess."

When I didn't speak, Ved continued.
"Tungar is not worthy to become a
general. He is unclean. He has touched
an Untouchable!"

The other soldiers gasped.

Asoka's expression did not change.

"I saw Tungar and Nandi saving a little boy from falling over a cliff. And the little boy was an Untouchable," Ved explained.

Asoka frowned and walked toward us.

Nandi hid behind me. But I stood tall and straight like a general.

"There is the Untouchable." Ved pointed at the boy without looking at him.

Asoka looked down at the boy. "Come out from under the bush," he ordered.

The little boy crawled out. His hair was covered in leaves, and his face was dirty.

"Is this story true?" Asoka asked.

The boy did not look at Asoka. He knew it was wrong to speak to members of other castes.

Asoka knelt next to the boy and touched his shoulder. General Talik rushed to stop him. But Asoka brushed the general away. "I am Buddhist. The castes don't matter to me anymore."

Asoka turned back to the boy. "Is it true?" he repeated.

The little boy nodded.

Asoka patted the boy on the head. Then he turned to me.

"I didn't know he was an Untouchable!" I explained.

Asoka looked at Nandi. "Did you know?"

Nandi nodded. "Yes. I knew. But I couldn't let him die."

Asoka smiled. "Nandi is truly brave. He is a hero."

I was angry. "What about me? I saved them both!"

"And what about me?" Ved added. "Don't I deserve a reward for telling the truth?"

"You told the truth," said Asoka. "But you told it for the wrong reason."

Then Asoka looked at me. "Yes, you did save them, Tungar. And sometimes doing good is its own reward." Then Asoka turned and led Nandi away.

Nandi looked back at me. "You'll always be a general in my eyes, Tungar. And you'll always be my friend."

Nandi was no longer my puppy dog.

I smiled at him. Suddenly we had switched places. He used to look at me with admiring eyes. Now I was staring at him in admiration.

"Yes. We'll always be friends," I told him. And I knew it was true.

I had much to learn from Nandi. Maybe someday I would learn enough to become a general.

Afterword: Ancient Indian Religions

Hinduism was the major religion of ancient India. Hindu people, or Hindi, believed in the caste system. There were four castes, or classes, based on wealth, power, and occupation. Each caste had a set of rules to live by. Ancient Hindu people also believed in many gods.

The religion of Buddhism began in ancient India around 500 B.C. A young prince named Gautama Buddha (GOW-tah-mah BOO-duh) left his royal home to search for a solution to human sadness. Buddha discovered that desire is the cause of human sadness. Happiness could be found by giving up all desires. People who followed Buddha's teachings practiced peace and respect for all living things.

Buddhism spread slowly in ancient India. After King Asoka became Buddhist, he began sending people called missionaries throughout India. These missionaries spread the message of Buddhism. He also sent missionaries into China and other Asian kingdoms.

Many people began to follow Buddhism. The Hindu religion adopted some Buddhist views. Both Buddhists and Hindi respected each other's religions and lived together in peace.

Jainism (JINE-izm) is another religion that began in ancient India. Jainism influenced both the Hindu and the Buddhist religions. Ancient Jains (JINES) believed that people should respect all living beings, because all living beings have souls.

On the Web

FactHound offers a safe, fun way to find Web sites related to topics in this book. All of the sites on FactHound have been researched by our staff.

1. Visit *www.facthound.com*
2. Type in this special code: 140485228X
3. Click on the FETCH IT button.

Your trusty FactHound will fetch the best sites for you!

Look for more *Read-It!* Reader Chapter Books: Historical Tales: